IVANHOE

IVANHOE
By Sir Walter Scott

Adapted by Jan Gleiter
Illustrated by Rick Whipple

RSVP
RAINTREE
STECK-VAUGHN
PUBLISHERS
The Steck-Vaughn Company

Austin, Texas

Library of Congress Number: 88-27461

Library of Congress Cataloging-in-Publication Data

Gleiter, Jan, 1987-
  Ivanhoe / [adapted by] Jan Gleiter and Kathleen Thompson:
illustrated by Rick Whipple.

  SUMMARY: A simplified retelling of the adventures of the Saxon knight Ivanhoe in 1194, the year of Richard the Lion-Hearted's return from the Third Crusade.
  1. Great Britain—History—Richard I, 1189-1199—Juvenile fiction.
[1. Great Britain—History—Richard I, 1189-1199—Fiction.
2. Knights and knighthood—Fiction.] I. Thompson, Kathleen.
II. Whipple, Rick, ill. III. Scott, Walker, Sir 1771-1832. Ivanhoe. IV. Title.
PZ7.G4817Iv   1988   [Fic.]—dc19   88-27461

ISBN 0-8172-2765-2 hardcover library binding

ISBN 0-8114-6829-1 softcover binding

7 8 9 10 11   99 98

CONTENTS

CHAPTER I

During the reign of Richard I, while that noble king was held captive by the Duke of Austria, England and the English were in a sad condition. The nobles, who had long held great power, had seized even more while Richard the Lion-Hearted was away at the Crusades.

The people were in despair, oppressed by the nobles and threatened at every turn by the loss of their land and their freedom. The tyranny of the nobles and the suffering of the common people was due, in large part, to the results of the Norman Conquest. A hundred years before, Duke William of Normandy had invaded England and defeated the Saxon king, Harold II. The Saxons, who had conquered England in the fifth century, found themselves ruled and controlled in almost every way by the Normans.

In these ancient times, there extended a large forest covering most of the land watered by the river Don. This beautiful forest was the home of bands of gallant outlaws, whose deeds have been recorded in English song.

Through this forest, one evening, rode a group of horsemen. Two of the party were of obvious importance. One, Brian de Bois-Guilbert, was a knight who had recently returned from the Crusades in the Holy Land. He was one of a special order of knights, the Knights of the Temple, or Knights Templar. These knights supported Philip of France, an enemy of King Richard's. The other traveler was a worldly-minded churchman, Prior Aymer.

Both were seeking an estate called Rotherwood, the home of Cedric the Saxon, to find shelter for the night.

As they rode, they discussed Cedric. "He has a ward, a young woman by the name of Rowena," said the Prior. "She is as dear to him as if she were his own child. It is said that he banished his only son from his family because he showed affection towards this beauty. So watch what you say and do in Cedric's presence. The Lady Rowena may be worshipped but, it appears, only at a distance."

"You have said enough," said Bois-Guilbert. "I will, for a night, behave as meekly as a maiden."

With this agreement, the two continued until they came to a fork in the road. Here they disagreed about the correct direction to go. Neither could convince the other until a stranger who knew the way offered to guide them. When asked who he was, he described himself as a pilgrim, recently returned from the Holy Land, who was himself on his way to the dwelling of Cedric the Saxon.

When the travelers arrived, Cedric ordered that they be admitted and shown to the dining hall. He disliked Normans too strongly to find any pleasure in their company, but he was too hospitable to turn any traveler away.

Cedric was a broad-shouldered, powerfully built man with the kind of good-humored expression that is often paired with a sudden and violent temper. He had spent his life guarding the rights that he knew he might have to fight for at any moment.

Bois-Guilbert and the Prior were given seats near Cedric at the high table. The pilgrim who had guided them took a place at the lower table with the servants, where he was scarcely noticed. Shortly after they sat down, the Lady Rowena entered the hall and moved gracefully toward the high table. The Knight Templar stared at her in such fascination that she became uncomfortably aware of his gaze and pulled her veil across her face.

Cedric noticed the gesture and what had caused it. "Sir Knight," he said coldly, "the cheeks of our Saxon maidens

have seen too little of the sun to enable them to bear the fixed glance of a crusader."

"If I have offended, I beg your pardon," answered Bois-Guilbert. "That is, I beg the lady's pardon."

"The Lady Rowena," said the Prior, "has punished us all in scolding the boldness of my friend. But I hope she will be less cruel tomorrow and agree to join our group to travel to the tournament at Ashby. Surely you are going?"

"I do not love these events, which were unknown in the days when England was free," replied Cedric. "And if we do go, we will not need your protection. My good neighbor Athelstane and I will travel together, and we are fully able to defend ourselves against any robbers or dangers that might be present on the journey."

Conversation was here interrupted by a servant who announced that another traveler had arrived at the gates, an old Jew by the name of Isaac of York.

Bois-Guilbert, who was deeply prejudiced against the Jewish people, spoke up. "Surely you will not admit a Jew into our presence," he said haughtily.

"My hospitality is not controlled by your dislikes," answered Cedric. Then, turning to his servant, he ordered him to admit the stranger and show him to the dining hall.

A few moments later, a tall, thin, old man entered the hall. He was signaled to take a place at the lower table. But there was no room for him until the pilgrim stood and offered his own seat. The younger man then moved closer to the high table where he stood, listening quietly.

Rowena, who hungered for news from the Holy Land, asked Bois-Guilbert to tell her what he knew of the Crusades and the English fighting there. He willingly replied.

"King Richard brought with him many brave warriors," said Bois-Guilbert. "They were second only to . . ."

"None!" interrupted the pilgrim. "They were second to none who ever drew sword! King Richard himself and five of his knights held a tournament one day. On that

9

day, the king and his knights offered to fight all challengers. Each of King Richard's knights defeated three opponents, all of whom were Knights of the Temple. Sir Brian de Bois-Guilbert knows well the truth of what I tell you."

It is impossible for language to describe the scowl of rage that passed over the Templar's face at hearing this description. But Cedric, who was gleeful at hearing of the glory of his countrymen, asked the pilgrim to name the knights who had performed so well. The pilgrim willingly named four, but hesitated at the name of the fifth.

"I will tell the name of the fifth knight," said Bois-Guilbert scornfully. "It was the Knight of Ivanhoe. None other was as skilled as he. Yet, if he were in England now, if he were to repeat his challenge at the tournament at Ashby, I would gladly fight him again. And win."

"Your challenge would be soon answered," replied the pilgrim, "if your enemy were near. If Ivanhoe ever returns from the Holy Land, I will make sure that he meets you."

The Lady Rowena listened to this conversation with the greatest interest while Cedric sat silently, a storm of mixed emotions showing in his expression.

The dinner then came to a close and the guests were shown to the rooms where they would spend the night. When the pilgrim reached his room, he asked where Isaac of York was sleeping and where he could find Gurth, the swineherd. The servant pointed out their rooms, and the pilgrim entered his own, where he promptly fell fast asleep.

When the earliest sunbeams found their way through his window, the pilgrim arose quickly and went immediately to the room of Isaac of York. He touched the sleeping old man with his staff to awaken him, whereupon Isaac started up with a look of wild surprise.

"Fear nothing from me, Isaac," said the pilgrim. "I come as your friend. When the Templar crossed the hall last night, he spoke to his slaves in their own language, which I understand. He told them to take the first opportunity to rob you."

"Holy God of Abraham!" exclaimed the old man. "What shall I do?"

"Leave this place immediately," the pilgrim continued. I will guide you by the secret paths of the forest. Follow me."

The pilgrim then led the way to the room occupied by Gurth the swineherd and ordered him to undo the gate to let them out. Gurth at first refused, but the pilgrim whispered into his ear. The swineherd then rose up, as if electrified, to do his bidding.

When Isaac and the pilgrim had safely arrived near the town of Sheffield where Isaac would be safe, the pilgrim attempted to take his leave.

"Not without my thanks," said Isaac.

"I desire nothing," replied the pilgrim. "I need nothing and want nothing."

"I must do something," said Isaac. "And I believe I know what you do need. Your wish is for a horse and armor. There were words from you last night that, like sparks from flint, showed the metal within. And hidden inside your pilgrim's gown is a knight's chain and spurs of gold. I saw them when you leaned over me this morning."

So saying, he gave the pilgrim a scroll and told him to take it to a rich Jew in Leicester. He, after reading what was written, would supply a war horse fit for a king and all the weapons and armor needed for a tournament. The two men then parted and went their separate ways.

CHAPTER II

While Richard the Lion-Hearted was imprisoned in Austria, his brother, Prince John, was trying his utmost to continue Richard's captivity. He plotted, with Philip of France, to keep Richard imprisoned. In the meantime, Prince John was doing all he could to increase his own power and influence in England.

Prince John was a conceited, sulky, suspicious, and cowardly man. But he was enormously sly. Many powerful men chose to support his goals in the hope that when he was crowned king, they would be rewarded.

The prince caused a great deal of distress in the minds and hearts of the English people, who loved their king but not his brother. Yet, there was one event that brought pleasure and excitement to rich and poor alike—the tournament. The one that was to take place at Ashby had attracted a great number of people who arrived, upon the appointed morning, at the place of combat.

Nobles and commoners, Normans and Saxons together filled the stands, shouting with excitement. In a section of special seats sat the greatest beauties of the land, one of whom would be chosen by the tournament's victor to be the Queen of Love and Beauty.

As the tournament was about to begin, Isaac of York made his way slowly to a seat in the front row. With him was his daughter, Rebecca, a young woman of such loveliness that she attracted the attention of everyone there and such lack of conceit that she was unaware of the effect she had. Rebecca had heard from her father about the young man who had saved him from robbery and certain death. She knew, also, of Isaac's gift of a horse and armor to this young man, and she watched eagerly for some sign of him.

The tournament was organized in such a way that five knights, the champions, were to be fought, one-on-one, by five challengers, who were all Normans. The leader of the challengers was Brian de Bois-Guilbert. Another was a neighbor and enemy of Cedric's, Reginald Front-de-Boeuf, whose name in the language of the Saxons meant "Ox-face."

As the trumpets blared, these two groups started out against each other at full gallop, each knight holding a long lance with which he hoped to knock his opponent from his horse. This event, the joust, was the only competition for the first day of the tournament, but it could easily go on for many hours as new knights appeared to compete with the earlier winners.

As the dust cleared after the first attack, it was clear that the challengers were the victors. All five had defeated the champions they fought. Five new knights took the champions' places, then five more and five more. But not one of the Norman challengers fell from his horse or swerved from the attack.

Cedric the Saxon, who had come to the tournament in the company of his young friend Athelstane was bitterly disappointed. He saw each triumph of the Normans as a triumph over the honor of England.

After the fourth group of knights had challenged the Normans, it appeared that no one else was ready to face such sure defeat. There was quite a long pause in the activity, and Prince John began to talk about preparing the banquet for that night. It seemed that the prize for the day's events would be awarded to Brian de Bois-Guilbert, who had done the best of all. Then, as the challengers' music ended, it was answered by a single trumpet. Each

eye turned to see the new knight that these sounds announced as he rode slowly towards the jousting field.

Rebecca's heart thrilled to see the newcomer. She knew at once that it was the man who had saved her father. He wore a magnificent suit of armor and rode a spirited black horse. On his shield was a young oak tree, pulled up by its roots, and the Spanish word *Desdichado*, meaning "disinherited." His grace and the skill with which he rode earned him the favor of the crowds and they called to him, "Choose Ralph de Vipont. He has the least skill. He is your best bargain."

But the Disinherited Knight rode straight up to Brian de Bois-Guilbert and struck his shield with his lance. This was the formal challenge, and Bois-Guilbert was quick to answer it.

"I hope you have said your confession and been to church this morning, brother," said the Templar. "For you shall sleep tonight in paradise."

"My gratitude for your courtesy," replied the newcomer. "I advise you to take a fresh horse and a new lance for, by my honor, you will need both."

He then positioned himself at the far end of the field and waited for Bois-Guilbert to mount and be ready. Few in the crowd believed for an instant that the Disinherited Knight could succeed, but his courage made him a favorite.

The trumpets had no sooner given the signal than the two knights urged their mounts into a gallop and rushed towards each other. They met in the center with the shock of a thunderbolt. Both lances burst into pieces, but neither knight lost his seating.

They returned to their places, received fresh lances, and the trumpets signaled another match. This time, the Disinherited Knight aimed his lance at his opponent's helmet, a much more difficult target than his shield. The force of the blow knocked the Templar to the ground.

"We shall meet again, I trust," said Bois-Guilbert bitterly.

"If we do not, the fault will not be mine," replied the

Disinherited Knight. He then commanded his trumpeter to sound the challenge to all of the victors.

One by one, knight after knight, the remaining four rode out against the stranger. One by one, they were defeated. The applause of thousands met the announcement that the day's honors went to the Disinherited Knight. He was brought forward to the prince's throne to receive his prize—a war-horse of incredible beauty and matchless strength.

"Sir Disinherited Knight," said Prince John, "since that is the only name we know to use for you, it is now your duty to name the fair lady, who, as Queen of Beauty and Love, will rule over tomorrow's events. Raise your lance."

He placed a narrow gold crown on the tip of the stranger's lance and watched as the young knight rode along the stands to where the Lady Rowena was seated. He stood silently before her and then, at her feet, he dropped the crown. A shout went up from the crowd, "Long live the Lady Rowena! Long live the Saxon princess!" The knight then rode out of the arena.

The next morning, the tournament continued. The contest this day was between large groups of knights, fifty to a side. The Disinherited Knight led one side; Brian de Bois-Guilbert led the other. Cedric's friend Athelstane decided to fight on the side of the Templar. He had been angered by the Disinherited Knight's attention to Rowena, whom Athelstane greatly admired.

The two groups galloped towards each other, meeting in the middle with a crashing shock. Many were knocked from their horses and continued to fight from the ground. Some lay stretched on the ground as if they would never rise. Some were stopping their blood with scarves and trying to get out of the tangle of men and horses. In the meantime, the clanging noises of the swords and the shouts of the fighting knights drowned the groans of those who fell and rolled beneath the feet of the horses.

As the fighting continued, those who watched shouted and cheered. "Fight on, brave knights! Man dies, but glory lives! Fight on—death is better than defeat!"

In the midst of the fighting, the Disinherited Knight and Bois-Guilbert tried to single each other out. The fall of either one would mean that the other side had won, but neither had yet fallen. Finally, the leaders met and attacked each other with such strength and skill that the spectators broke forth in shouts of admiration.

It so happened that, at this time, the Disinherited Knight's side had the worst of it. The gigantic Front-de-Boeuf and the huge strength of Athelstane had given the Templar's side an advantage. It now occurred to these two knights that they could help their side the most by joining Bois-Guilbert in his fight with the Disinherited Knight. And so they turned, as one, upon him. The Disinherited Knight could not have survived the attack if he had not been warned by a cry from the spectators.

"Beware, Sir Disinherited!" they shouted, so loudly that he became aware of the danger and pulled back his horse just in time. But the attackers wheeled around, and now all three pursued him with vigor. Nothing could have saved him, except the remarkable strength of the noble horse which he had won on the day before. The animal's ability and its rider's skill allowed him to keep his attackers away for a few moments. But it was clear that he could not succeed for long.

There was, among the ranks of the Disinherited Knight, a large, powerful man in black armor, mounted on a black horse. Throughout the fighting, he had easily beaten off anyone who attacked him, but he had shown little interest in the fighting and had not, himself, attacked anyone.

Now, the Black Knight saw the leader of his side in great danger and rode to his side like lightning. He struck Front-de-Boeuf a tremendous blow, knocking him to the ground. He then turned and pulled Athelstane's battle-ax from his hand, using that weapon to strike its former owner on the helmet. The Black Knight then returned to his previous attitude of disinterest and rode calmly to the side of the field, leaving his leader to deal with

Bois-Guilbert.

The Disinherited Knight, who no longer had to deal with three opponents, charged the Templar and knocked him from his horse. Leaping to the ground, he drew his sword and demanded that Bois-Guilbert give up the fight. Prince John, seeing this and wanting to save the Templar from humiliation, ended the fight.

Four knights had died on the field. Thirty were badly wounded, and four or five of these later died from their wounds. The survivors carried the marks of the conflict to their graves. And thus ended what has been recorded in history as the Gentle and Joyous Tournament of Ashby.

Prince John, who did not want to give the Disinherited Knight another victory, tried to award the day's prize to the Black Knight. But he had disappeared, riding off into the forest. And so the Disinherited Knight was brought before the Lady Rowena to be crowned the victor.

As he stood before her, his helmet was lifted from his head by the attendants. Upon seeing the sunburned face of the young knight, Rowena let out a shriek. Cedric also recognized immediately that the victor was his son, Wilfred the Knight of Ivanhoe.

The knight stooped to kiss Rowena's hand, but fell to the ground in a faint. When his armor was removed, it was revealed that the point of a lance had been driven into his side.

CHAPTER III

As soon as the name Ivanhoe was uttered, the news of it flew from spectator to spectator. Prince John had heard of the Knight of Ivanhoe and his loyalty to King Richard. He was greatly displeased at this enemy's success in the tournament.

One of the prince's advisers now approached the royal party. "The gallant Ivanhoe is not likely to disturb your highness in any way," he said. "He is badly wounded and has been carried off by his friends."

Prince John then turned his attention to a question he had about the Queen of Love and Beauty. "Who is this Lady Rowena," he asked, "who was so saddened by the wounds that Ivanhoe received?"

"She is a Saxon heiress," replied one of the prince's attendants. "She is a rose of loveliness and a jewel of wealth."

"Then let us marry her to a Norman," said the prince. "She is surely young enough to be considered a minor and could, therefore, be forced to do my royal bidding in terms of a marriage."

He turned to one of his young knights. "What say you, De Bracy, to the idea of gaining more land and wealth by wedding a Saxon?" This idea was, of course, perfectly agreeable to De Bracy who had been greatly impressed with the loveliness of the lady.

At this point, a note was put into Prince John's hands.

"It is from foreign parts, my lord, but I do not know from whom it comes," said his attendant.

The prince broke the seal and read the note. He grew as pale as death upon seeing the words it contained—

"Take heed to yourself, for the Devil is unchained!"

Upon recovering from his first surprise, the prince took his adviser and De Bracy aside. "It means," he said, showing them the note, "that my brother Richard has obtained his freedom. It is written in Philip of France's own handwriting."

"We must return as quickly as possible to York, or some other central place, and make arrangements to set the crown of England upon Prince John's head," said the adviser. "But the country folk will be dissatisfied if they think that their fun has been cut short. Let us end the activities with an archery contest and then be done with it."

"Yes," agreed John. "I have already told a certain rude peasant that he would have to compete in an archery contest. He had the nerve to be quite bold in speaking to me the other day. And he bragged that he could win whatever contest I set for him. I would get my vengeance on him even if this were my last hour of power."

So saying, he commanded that all archers who wished to compete should now enter the field. More than thirty wanted at first to try their skill. But when they saw the others, all excellent shots, only eight remained. Prince John then looked for the man who had angered him and found him where he had been the day before.

"What is thy name, archer?" he asked.

"Locksley," replied the man.

"Well, Locksley, you shall shoot when the others have displayed their skill. You must beat the best of them, or you will be banished from this place."

"This I will do," replied Locksley, "if after two shots at your target, I can choose the target for the last shot."

Prince John agreed. The eight archers then each shot three arrows. The two arrows closest to the center of the target were those of a woodsman named Hubert.

Since Hubert had won, he shot first in the contest against Locksley. He raised his bow and studied the target for a great while. Then, drawing in his breath, he released the arrow, which hit very near the center of the target. Locksley then stepped forward, raised his bow carelessly, and let fly an arrow that pierced the target two inches closer to the center.

For the second shot, Hubert took even greater care. This time his arrow hit the exact center. Locksley again raised his bow. This time, he paid more attention. When he released his arrow, it splintered Hubert's in two.

The crowd was so astonished that it was almost silent. "Such archery has never been seen," whispered the archers to each other.

"And now," said Locksley, "I will choose a target."

He selected a slender stalk of willow, about as big around as a man's thumb, and stuck it into the ground at the far end of the field. "To ask a good woodsman to shoot at a great, broad target is an insult," he said. "He might as well shoot at King Arthur's round table. A child of seven could hit such a target as has been used here. But this target will test a man's skill."

"Not mine," replied Hubert. "I might as well shoot at a sunbeam. I will not shoot at what I am sure to miss."

Locksley raised his bow. He then took aim with great care while the crowd waited in breathless silence. He let loose the arrow, which split the willow in two.

Prince John was overcome with amazement. He forgot for a moment his anger at this archer. "I will increase your prize greatly," he said, "if you will enter my service as an archer with my guards."

"I have vowed," replied Locksley, "that if ever I do such a thing, it will be in service only with your royal brother, King Richard."

He then assured Hubert that he would have hit willow if he had tried, disappeared into the crowd, and was gone.

CHAPTER IV

The next day, Prince John began to work even harder to gain the support of any knights and nobles who hesitated in making a choice between him and Richard. He intended to have himself crowned king within a very short while and to justify this action as the result of popular demand.

In the meantime, De Bracy had a plan of his own, which had nothing to do with Prince John's goal of the throne of England. Disguised as the outlaws who lived in the forests, he and his men would kidnap the Lady Rowena and the group with which she was returning to Rother-wood. Then, while she was imprisoned in Front-de-Boeuf's castle, he would find a way to make her agree to marry him. And so, dressed in forest green and wearing a leather cap, he set off.

Now, as the reader may recall, the man called the Black Knight had ridden off at the end of the tournament, as soon as the victory was clear. He had started out on quite a long journey through the forest. By the time that De Bracy was making his plan, the Black Knight was quite hopelessly lost in the tangled paths of the woods and began to look, rather anxiously, for some sign of a cottage where he might find food and rest. By evening, he let go of the reins of his horse in the hope that the good animal would have better luck in finding somewhere for them to stay.

The knight's horse chose a path that was not as well worn as the others and soon stopped in front of a rough cottage. This hut had a piece of wood tied across a small tree near the door, as a symbol of the holy cross. It appeared to be some sort of small chapel or the home of a hermit as, indeed, it proved to be. The Black Knight banged on the door with his lance, sure that the resident of such a place would be happy to supply his needs. But the response from inside was not encouraging.

"Pass on, whoever you are," was the answer to his knock. "Do not disturb the servant of God in his prayers. I have nothing that even a dog would want to share. So pass on, and God speed thee."

"Pass on, how?" replied the knight. "Tell me, at least, how to find the road, if I can expect nothing else from you."

"The road," replied the hermit's voice, "is easy to find. Take this path to the swamp. From there, continue to the ford, which may be passable now that the rain has stopped. Then climb the left bank of the cliff carefully, as it is rather dangerous, and take the path which hangs over the river and often gives way in various places. Then continue straight forward . . ."

"A broken path, a cliff, a ford, and a swamp!" interrupted the knight. "I say, open this door, holy father, or I will beat it down!"

The hermit, realizing he had no choice, opened the door and admitted the knight. For quite a while, he pretended that, as he had claimed, he had nothing but dry grain and water to offer. However, as the two men talked, the knight's open friendliness and humor became clear to the hermit, and he brought out a huge meat pie and a large leather bottle of wine.

The two became quite friendly indeed and drank and sang the night away. They were quite busy with their laughter and songs when they were interrupted by a loud knocking at the door of the hut. To explain this knocking, it is necessary to leave the hermit and the knight and to resume the adventures of another of our characters.

It was Cedric the Saxon's strongest desire to see his people free themselves from their Norman rulers. His friend and neighbor, Athelstane, was descended from a noble Saxon line. For this reason, Cedric had decided long ago that he and Rowena, who was descended from the last Saxon king, should marry. Athelstane found this plan agreeable, but Rowena did not have the same reaction. She was in love with Wilfred of Ivanhoe and was not even particularly fond of Athelstane.

The sudden appearance of his son at the tournament seemed to deal a death blow to Cedric's hopes. Even so, he still felt a great deal of fatherly affection for the young man, despite the problems between them. And so, when he saw his son collapse, he ordered a servant to keep an eye on him and to remove him, as soon as possible, for care. However, when the crowd had cleared out, the Knight of Ivanhoe was nowhere to be seen. The few remaining spectators said that he had been carried off, quite gently, and placed in a cart belonging to a lady.

Cedric had been extremely worried about his son, but as soon as he heard that that he was in careful hands, his attitude changed. "Let that disobedient young man go wherever he wishes, with whomever he pleases," he said. "We must leave at sunrise for Rotherwood."

The next morning, Cedric, Athelstane, and the rest of their party began their journey home. At the edge of the wooded country that the group had to pass through to reach home, they heard cries for assistance. They were surprised to find Isaac of York, his daughter, and a cart with a wounded man. Isaac told the story of how they had hired bodyguards in Ashby to escort them home. But when they had received news that a band of outlaws was waiting in the woods, the bodyguards had taken their horses and left the travelers with no defense or means of transporting their friend.

Rowena urged Cedric to allow Isaac, Rebecca, and their sick friend to join them, and the larger group started into the forest. As they hurried along the narrow path, De

Bracy and his men, disguised as outlaws, sprang from behind the trees and attacked them. Cedric and his companions did not have a chance to overcome their attackers and were quickly taken as prisoners. Gurth, who was riding with the group, and Wamba, Cedric's jester, were the only ones who escaped into the woods. As these two servants hid among the trees, another man dressed in forest green appeared before them. At first, they were terrified, but the man assured them that he was not with the attackers.

"My name is Locksley," said he. "My men and I dwell in these woods and many call us outlaws. But capturing women is not one of our tricks. Wait here."

He went off to mingle among the attackers and returned shortly. "I have learned where they are going," said Locksley. "To the castle of Reginald Front-de-Boeuf. There is nothing that only three of us can do. But I can soon gather such a force as may deal with these people. Cedric the Saxon is a friend of the rights of Englishmen. It will not be difficult to find men to fight to free him."

He then started off quickly through the woods, with Gurth and Wamba close behind. After three hours' walk, they arrived at a clearing in the woods where some of Locksley's men were gathered.

"Where is the Friar?" asked Locksley.

"At home, in his cottage," answered one of the men.

"I will go and get him," said Locksley. "Gather as many men as you can. There is game afoot that must be hunted hard. Meet me here by daybreak."

Locksley and his two companions then departed for the little chapel previously mentioned, and it was their knocking at the door that interrupted the songs of the hermit and his guest. The Friar and the Black Knight quickly agreed to fight to free Cedric and his party.

CHAPTER V

While these things were being done in behalf of Cedric and his companions, the armed men who had captured them hurried to Front-de-Boeuf's castle. Once inside, the captives were separated into various rooms. Rowena was left alone in one room, Rebecca was taken to another, Isaac was dragged off to the dungeon, and Cedric and Athelstane were imprisoned in what had once been the great hall of the castle.

Cedric paced the room and raved angrily while Athelstane complained chiefly about the rudeness of their captors in failing to supply a noon meal promptly. They were both surprised by the blast of a horn sounded from the front gate. It was repeated three times. No matter how they strained to see out the window, however, they could see only the courtyard.

Leaving the Saxon chiefs alone for a moment, we will look in upon the more severe imprisonment of Isaac of York. The old man had been thrown into the deep, damp dungeon of the castle. At one end of the room was a large fire-grate, with bars over the top. Isaac sat on the cold stones of this vault for nearly three hours until Reginald Front-de-Boeuf entered with two servants and placed a large set of scales in front of the unhappy man.

"On these very scales you will weigh me out one thousand pounds of silver," demanded Front-de-Boeuf. "Or you shall lie on those iron bars above a bed of glowing charcoal and be roasted alive."

"It is impossible that you can mean this," cried the miserable prisoner. "Whoever heard of a sum as huge as that! The good God of nature never made a heart that could do something so cruel!"

"You can easily get that amount from your people," said Front-de-Boeuf angrily. "Choose between your money and your life." He signaled his servants to start the fire and to drag Isaac to it.

"Let my daughter Rebecca go forth safely," replied the old man. "As soon as man and horse can return, the treasure will be yours."

"Impossible," said Front-de-Boeuf coldly. "I have already given your daughter to Sir Brian de Bois-Guilbert. He finds her quite attractive, and she is to be his."

The yell which Isaac let forth caused the walls of the dungeon to ring. "Then, robber and villain, I will pay you nothing! Take my life if you will, but not one silver penny will I pay you unless my daughter is delivered to me in safety and honor!"

"Then feel the fire!" said Front-de-Boeuf and commanded his servants to place him on the bars.

At this very moment, the faint sound of a bugle was heard in the dungeon, and voices rang out calling for Sir Reginald Front-de-Boeuf. Leaving Isaac alone, and for the moment safe, the savage Baron left the dungeon with his attendants.

While these things were going on, Rowena was busy convincing De Bracy that she would never marry him. De Bracy was not easily convinced.

"Ah, but you must," said he, "or all who are our prisoners will die, including your guardian Cedric and the Knight of Ivanhoe."

"Ivanhoe!" exclaimed Rowena. "But he is not here!"

"Yes, my lady," replied De Bracy. "The wounded man with Isaac of York and his daughter was, and is, none other than Ivanhoe. He is now our prisoner and will die with the others. Only you can save him."

This news, and the decision it forced upon Rowena, caused her such distress that she burst into tears. De Bracy could not bear to watch the lovely young woman in such misery and left her chamber, discouraged but still determined that he would eventually have his way.

Rebecca had to deal with a harder heart than De Bracy's. Sir Brian de Bois-Guilbert declared straight out that, although his vows as a Knight of the Temple prevented him from marrying, he intended that Rebecca would become his lover.

"You are the captive of my bow and spear," said Bois-Guilbert. "I can take by force what I am not freely given."

"Stand back!" cried Rebecca. She flung open the window of her room and leaped out upon the wall, high above the courtyard below. "If you come one step closer, I will plunge from this height and die on the stones below!"

The Templar was moved by this display and overcome with admiration of the beautiful young woman's bravery.

"You are the ideal woman of my heart's desire," he said, with genuine feeling. "In you, I have found the woman to share my life and my ambitions. Mine you must be, but only with your own consent and on your own terms. You have nothing to fear from me."

He was here interrupted by the sound of a bugle, blowing from the gate.

"That bugle sound announces something that may require my presence," said Bois-Guilbert. "Think about what I have said. I will soon return." With that, he left the room.

The bugle that had ended, for the moment, the torments of several of the captives, had been blown by one of Locksley's men at the gate. He brought a demand that the prisoners be freed. It was answered only by a note from Bois-Guilbert saying that a priest should be sent to hear the prisoners' confessions before they were put to death. This reply convinced the Black Knight and Locksley that they must attack the castle, and do so soon.

The knights within the castle laughed at the idea that they were in any danger from mere archers outside their walls.

"Those stingless pests!" they said impatiently. "They could never take this castle! They have no battering rams, no ladders, no experienced leaders! Even with most of our men away at York with Prince John, those fools cannot threaten us."

Nonetheless, they immediately began to send men to the tops of the wall to defend the castle from attack.

Rebecca, who had been moved into Ivanhoe's chamber to care for him, could hear the heavy tramp of feet running along the passages and up the stairs which led to the various points of defense. Her eyes burned with an emotion that was half terror and half a thrilling hope.

Ivanhoe could also hear and was nearly mad with impatience and frustration at not being able to join the battle. To calm him, Rebecca stood at the window, despite danger from arrows and rocks, and described what she could see of the preparations for the fight. She told him of the Black Knight, whom she could see leading the attack, and of the archers that filled the woods.

"Now there is a cloud of arrows, flying so thick as to dazzle my eyes," she exclaimed. "And the Black Knight is leading a group of attackers to the outer wall. Front-de-Boeuf leads the defenders. They rush in. They are thrust back. They come again! It is the meeting of two fierce tides! Now Front-de-Boeuf and the Black Knight fight hand to hand, amid the roar of their followers! Front-de-Boeuf is down, felled by a mighty blow! His men drag him back within the walls. The attackers have taken the outer wall!"

The battle went on, starting and stopping, now with the attackers gaining ground and then with the defenders succeeding. At last there came a pause in which everyone rested and planned the next attack or defense.

As the Black Knight prepared to lead a new attack and Locksley positioned his archers, suddenly smoke was seen, billowing from the castle towers. An old Saxon woman within the castle had finally seen her chance to get revenge on the Normans who had stolen the castle and murdered her family many years before. She had lit a fire, and now she danced among the flames and smoke, singing an old Saxon chant.

In the chamber where Rebecca tended Ivanhoe, smoke began to roll in under the door. "The castle burns," said Rebecca. "It burns! What can we do to save ourselves?"

"Fly, Rebecca, and save your own life," said Ivanhoe. "For no human aid can save me."

At this moment, the door of the chamber burst open and the Templar appeared. He grabbed up Rebecca to take her to safety.

"Savage warrior!" said Rebecca. "I would rather perish in the flames than accept safety from you!"

But Bois-Guilbert paid no attention to her objections and, leaving Ivanhoe alone and helpless, carried her out.

In the meantime, the Black Knight had succeeded in gaining entrance through the castle gate. He fought his way along the passages, leaving the castle defenders dead and dying in his wake. He burst through the door to Ivanhoe's room and carried him out with as much ease as the Templar had carried Rebecca.

While Rowena and the other prisoners were being rescued, the battle continued in the courtyard. Bois-Guilbert fought like a madman, neglecting his own defense to assure Rebecca's safety. Then, seeing that the battle was lost, he put spurs to his horse and rode out of the castle with Rebecca as his captive.

CHAPTER VI

In a clearing in the forest, the freed prisoners gathered with the outlaw band, the Black Knight, and the captured De Bracy. Here, with every fairness, Locksley divided the wealth that had been taken from the ruined castle. The Black Knight asked for only one thing—the right to determine De Bracy's fate. Granted this request, he freed De Bracy. The Black Knight then took his leave, after being presented with a bugle that Locksley assured him would bring him and his men at a run, if it were blown.

De Bracy, who had been told the Black Knight's identity by that noble warrior himself, rode straight to Prince John. At the Castle of York, he presented himself to John and his chief adviser.

"The Templar has fled," said De Bracy. "Front-de-Boeuf you will see no more. He has found a red death among the blazing rafters of his own castle. I alone have escaped to tell you. But the worst news is this. Richard is in England. I have seen and spoken with him."

Prince John turned pale, tottered, and caught at a bench to support himself. "He must be captured and imprisoned!" said the prince. "Go at once, with as much help as you require, to accomplish this!" he commanded.

"Not I," refused De Bracy. "I was his prisoner, and he took mercy on me. I will not harm him."

"I will go at once, my lord," said John's adviser. After gathering five of England's best archers, he set out to do the prince's bidding, riding fast for the forest where the Black Knight had last been seen.

While these things were going on, Rebecca was in even greater peril than when the flames had licked outside her chamber door. She was a prisoner at the estate of the Knights Templar. Although Bois-Guilbert did her no physical harm, he would not release her. When she was discovered by the head of the Templars, her situation was dangerous indeed. Like monks, the Knights Templar were supposed to be pure in mind and deed.

"She has charmed a Knight Templar," declared the head of the Templars. "Bois-Guilbert is helpless, caught in a mad passion for a Jew! The woman must be a witch, and we will prove it to save the reputation of our order!"

A trial was held immediately. All the good deeds that the good and gentle Rebecca had ever done in healing the sick and caring for the injured were used against her, as proof of witchcraft. Witnesses were called who told of Rebecca's amazing powers of healing, of the strangely sweet songs she sang, of the oddness of her dress, and of the unknown letters that were embroidered on her veil. One witness said that he had seen her perch upon the edge of the wall at Front-de-Boeuf's castle and then turn into a milk-white swan and fly three times around the tower.

Rebecca said that she had been taught healing skills as a young child. She explained that she dressed in the normal way for young Jewish women. She pointed out that the letters embroidered on her veil were Hebrew letters, strange only to Christians. But the court was determined to find her guilty and to burn her at the stake.

"Then I have but one chance for life by your own fierce laws," said Rebecca. "I deny this charge. I claim my innocence. I demand the right of trial by combat."

In those long-ago days, such a demand could be made. If a knight could be found to fight for the accused, he was considered to be her champion. If the champion won the combat, it was believed that God had protected the innocent. If he lost, it was believed that God had determined the guilt of the accused, and the witch was then burned at the stake.

"And who, Rebecca, will fight to the death for a witch, for a Jew?" asked the judge.

"God will raise me up a champion," said Rebecca. "There must be one who will fight for justice."

Rebecca spoke bravely, but her heart was heavy. The only knight that might fight for her, the Knight of Ivanhoe, was still recovering from serious wounds. And she did not know for certain that he would risk his life, even if he were well enough to try.

Bois-Guilbert was also desperately worried. He had been chosen to fight against Rebecca's champion, if one could be found. While Rebecca's father rode out in search of Ivanhoe, Bois-Guilbert tried one last time to convince her of his devotion. On the morning scheduled for the combat, he came to her in her cell.

"If I appear to fight your champion, whomever he may be, he will die quickly and you will die slowly, a most terrible death," began Bois-Guilbert. "But if I do not appear, you will live. I will lose honor and the possibility of greatness. I will be humiliated and disgraced."

The Templar looked steadily at the beautiful young woman, his eyes burning. "But I am willing to sacrifice everything to save you," he declared. "I risked my life to save you when the castle burned. I risked it again during the battle in the courtyard. Now, I will give up everything I have to save you once more, if you will be mine. You must flee with me to distant lands and be mine forever."

"It is only because of you that my life was ever in danger!" replied Rebecca with honest and heartfelt anger. "You captured me and dragged me to the castle! It was against my wishes that you carried me from the burning chamber! Now you offer to save me from a fate that you yourself have caused for me? No! The price you ask for my life is too high a price to pay. No!"

"Farewell, then," said the Templar, with a last long look, and he was gone.

While these terrible events were taking shape, the Black Knight was facing a conflict of his own. After taking the Knight of Ivanhoe to a small abbey to recover, he set off to gather a force of men. Ivanhoe and De Bracy knew his true identity, but he had revealed it to only a few others.

The Black Knight was well aware that if he rode into York and faced Prince John alone, he would, at best, spend the rest of his days in a prison cell. So, while the few he knew were loyal were raising an army, the Black Knight also went in search of warriors who would fight for his right to keep and wear the crown of England.

Deep in Sherwood Forest, the men sent by Prince John found the Black Knight. Five against one, they attacked. Five against one, they fought. Although the Black Knight swung his deadly sword with a skill and strength few men have ever had, he would have died among the trees but for the loyal friend he had in Locksley. Locksley and his men heard the Black Knight's bugle call for help. They raced to his aid and made short work of defeating Prince John's men.

The Black Knight turned to Locksley when the battle was over. "You have saved more than a friend, Locksley," he said. "You have saved your king."

And then, with a new majesty to his voice, he declared, "I am Richard of England."

The archer at once kneeled before him. "Call me Locksley no longer, my lord," he said. "Know me by the name that others—Robin Hood of Sherwood Forest."

"King of outlaws, and prince of good fellows," said the king. "Then my friend the priest must be Friar Tuck."

He looked around and found the cheerful friar, also on his knees. "You and your band of men have paid for all your crimes with the service you have given me. Arise, good fellows!" said Richard.

CHAPTER VII

Our story now returns to Rebecca at the hour when the bloody dice were to be cast to determine her fate. The estate of the Templars was prepared for the combat. The jousting field was ready. The stands were filled with spectators. Bois-Guilbert sat, pale as death, upon his war-horse. Rebecca stood by the stake where she was to burn.

No champion had appeared to fight for Rebecca's life, and it was the general belief that no one would. But the beautiful young woman's eyes remained steadfastly on the horizon except when they turned, now and then, towards heaven. Just as the trumpets sounded their last blast, a knight rode onto the field.

"A champion! A champion!" a hundred voices exclaimed. But it appeared that, although a champion had appeared, he would do little good for the unfortunate woman who stood at the stake. The knight's horse, who had galloped at full speed for many miles, seemed to stagger. The rider was barely able to remain in the saddle. Nonetheless, he declared his purpose in a strong, clear voice.

"I am Wilfred of Ivanhoe," said the knight, raising the visor of his helmet. Then, to Rebecca, "Do you accept me as your champion?"

"I do," she said. Then, looking carefully at him, she burst out, "No! Your wounds are still unhealed. Why should you die also?"

But Ivanhoe was already at his post and had closed his helmet and had taken up his lance. The trumpets sounded and the knights charged each other at full gallop. The wearied horse of Ivanhoe and its no less exhausted rider went down, as all had expected, before the well-aimed lance and strength of the Templar. But Bois-Guilbert, to the astonishment of all, reeled in his saddle, lost his stirrups, and fell to the ground.

Ivanhoe leaped up from the ground, put his sword to the fallen Templar's throat, and commanded him to yield or die. But Bois-Guilbert returned no answer. When his helmet visor was raised, his eyes were open, but they were fixed and glazed. Then they closed and the paleness of death passed over his face. Untouched by his enemy's lance, he had died a victim of the violence of his own warring passions.

"I will not take his weapons," said the Knight of Ivanhoe. "God's arm, and no human hand, has struck him down."

He was interrupted by the clattering of horses' feet, advancing in such number that the ground shook under them. The Black Knight and a large number of men rode onto the field. Richard the Lion-Hearted was now ready to declare his return. He rode, alone, up and down in front of the Templars.

"Will none of you dare to splinter a lance with me?" asked the king. "You were well prepared to fight against me while I was helplessly imprisoned in Austria. You worked to help my enemy, Philip of France, while I was gone. Do none of you wish to fight against me now, gallant knights?"

But there was no resistance to Richard. The rebels at the Castle of York had given up in the face of the forces Richard had raised. Prince John had fled to the safety of his mother's house, believing, correctly, that his brother would never raise a hand against his own mother's son. The struggle for the throne of England was over and

Richard the Lion-Hearted wore the crown.

When Cedric the Saxon received the news that his friend and rescuer, the Black Knight, was actually Richard of England, he realized that his dream of creating a Saxon rule was doomed. Then, with a reasonable amount of good grace, he agreed to give his blessing to the wedding of his son and the Lady Rowena.

Two days after that happy event, the Lady Rowena received a visitor. It was Rebecca.

"Please accept this small gift," said Rebecca, with quiet dignity, placing a priceless necklace in Rowena's hands. "Your husband saved my life. This is but a small gesture towards repaying the debt I owe the Knight of Ivanhoe. Please tell him of my gratitude and that I came to say good-bye."

Rowena could see how important it was to Rebecca that she accept the gift. "I accept it, with gratitude," she said. "But I know full well that it is he and I who owe you for the care you gave him him when he was desperately wounded. Now, tell me, why do you say good-bye?"

"The people of England are a fierce race," replied Rebecca. "This land is not safe land for the children of Israel. My father and I are leaving for a safer place, if there is such a place for my people. Farewell. May He who made both Jew and Christian shower down upon you his blessings." And, so saying, she glided from the room.

Rebecca's wish was granted. Ivanhoe and his lady lived long and happily. Ivanhoe served his king with honor and dignity. And, during his lifetime, the two races of Saxons and Normans mixed and married and began to blend in such a way that the angry differences between the two people seems, in these times, to have entirely disappeared.

GLOSSARY

archer (ärch′ ər) a person who is skilled in the use of a bow and arrow

battle-ax (bat′ əl aks) a large ax, also called a broadax, that was once used as a weapon of war

Crusades (kroo sādz′) in the eleventh, twelfth, and thirteenth centuries, military attempts by Christian powers to take the Holy Land from the Muslims

dungeon (dən′ jən) a dark prison that is usually underground

Norman Conquest (nòr′ mən kän′ kwest) the conquest of England in 1066 by the French and the Normans, who originally had come to Normandy from Scandanavia

lance (lans) a long spear that was carried by knights on horseback

Saxon (sak′ sən) one of the Germanic peoples that conquered England — with the Angles and the Jutes — in the fifth century

scroll (skrōl) a long roll of parchment, leather, paper, etc., used to write documents

swineherd (swīn′ herd) a person who tends swine